Grandma's Wheelchair

Lorraine Henriod · Pictures by Christa Chevalier

ALBERT WHITMAN & COMPANY, CHICAGO

Library of Congress Cataloging in Publication Data

Henriod, Lorraine.
   Grandma's wheelchair.

   (Concept books: Level 1)
   Summary: Four-year-old Thomas spends his mornings
helping his grandmother who is in a wheelchair.
   [1. Physically handicapped—Fiction. 2. Grandmothers—
Fiction] I. Chevalier, Christa, ill. II. Title
III. Series.
PZ7.H3934Gr   [E]   81-12918
ISBN 0-8075-3035-2 (lib. bdg.)   AACR2

The text of this book is set in eighteen point Baskerville.

To Nathaniel, Thomas, and Sarah

My brother, Nate, is five years old.
In the morning he puts on his blue sweater
and goes to kindergarten.

I am four years old. In the morning
I put on my red sweater and run
down the sidewalk to Grandma's house.

Nate thinks he's smart because he paints at an easel
and builds with blocks and plays games at kindergarten.

Grandma says I'm smart because I do
so many things to help her every day.
And I get to sit on her lap as long as I want.

I go in the back door at Grandma's house.
I take off my sweater and put it in the closet.
Grandma says, "We must call your mother
and let her know that you got here safe and sound."
She telephones my house. "Thomas is here with me,"
she says to my mom.

Then I talk to Mom. "See you later," I say.

I think, after my mom hangs up the phone,
she lies down for a while.
She lies down a lot.
She's getting rested before our new baby comes.

Sometimes Mom used to sit in a chair and
hold me on her lap after her work was done,
but she doesn't have much lap anymore.
Grandma always has a lap.
She sits in a chair all the time.

I climb up on Grandma's lap.
She reads me a story,
sometimes two stories.
Then we do her work, together.

Grandma has already cooked a pan full of apple slices.
Now I get to mash the apples into applesauce.
I like to eat applesauce for my lunch.

My blue hippopotamus stands
on the drainboard, watching me.
Oops! He falls into the applesauce, headfirst.
His face looks icky. He is a messy eater!
Pieces of apple are sticking to his nose and mouth,
so I wash him clean.

When the applesauce is done, Grandma says,
"I think the clothes are dry."
She pulls them out of the dryer and puts them,
all warm and soft, on top of me.
We wheel over to the table and fold them and put them
in piles.

First we take a pile of towels into the bathroom.
Dish towels go into the kitchen,
clean socks and underwear into the bedroom.

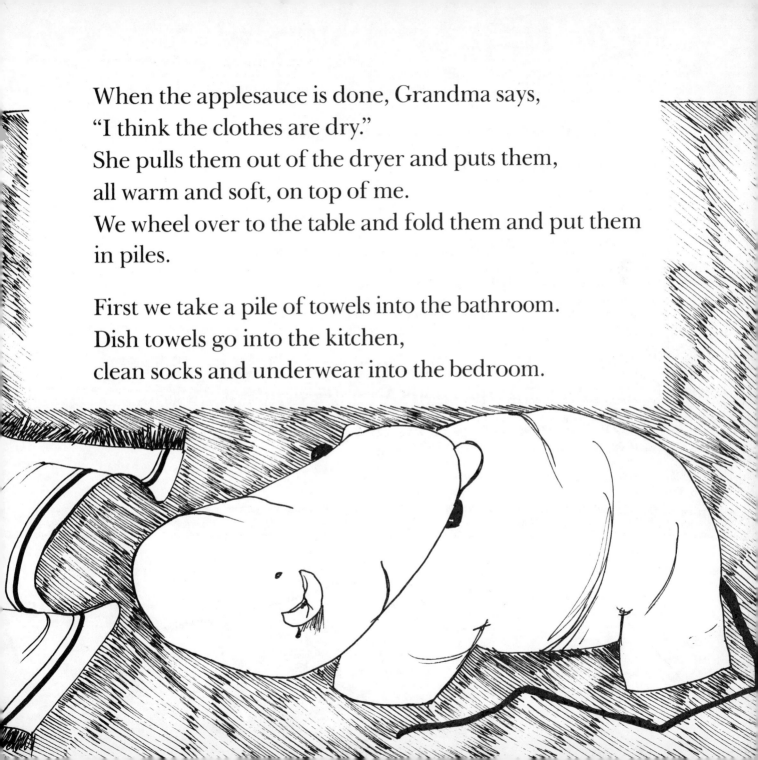

After the clothes are put away, I say,
"It's time to dust."

"You're right, Thomas." Grandma gets her
dust rag. She dusts almost everything.
But she can't reach the top of the bookcase,
so I stand on her lap and dust up there.

Oh, oh! My blue hippopotamus falls to the floor
when I dust the shelf. A lot of sawdust comes out
of the hole in his head and goes all over the floor.

"Never mind," Grandma says. "We'll get the vacuum."
The vacuum is heavy, but we pull it into the living room.
We are strong, Grandma and me, together.
She plugs it in, and I turn it on.

The vacuum goes "Brrr" while it is sucking up the sawdust.
After it has finished, we put it away.

"Let's go outside and wait for Nate," I say.
We wheel out the back door and swoosh
down a little hill onto the driveway.
Grandma and I like to go fast.
But today the wheelchair stops on the driveway
and doesn't move anymore.

Grandma pushes on the wheels,
and we go forward, very slowly.
We look down.

One of the big tires looks funny.
It has a twisted, puffy spot that sticks out.

"Oh, no!" Grandma says. "My wheelchair
has a blowout. We can't go fast until it is fixed."

"Will Grandpa fix it?"

"Yes, when he gets home from work.
Can you push me back to the house, Thomas?"

I climb down and start pushing.
Grandma tries to turn the wheels at the same time.

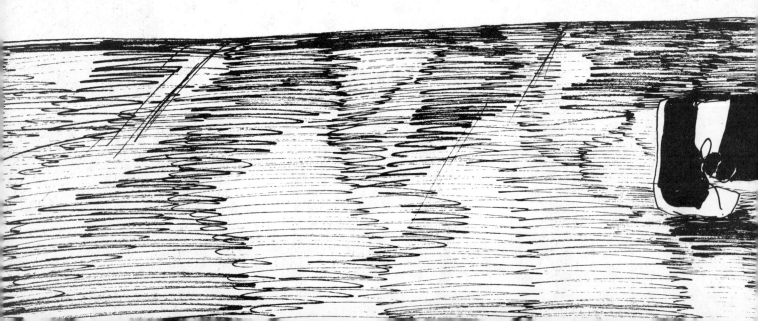

Pretty soon I am out of breath.
"I wish you had another wheelchair, Grandma."

"Why, Thomas, I do have another one.
I had forgotten all about it.
It's in the garage.
It's old, but it isn't broken, like this one."

Grandma's garage is full of interesting things.

I look behind some garbage cans
and see the Christmas wreath for Grandma's
front door. I look behind the lawn mower.
There's a doghouse and a bird cage!
I look behind a hoe and a rake and a wheelbarrow.
Then I see something with wheels, behind a ladder.

PAINT

The ladder is heavy, but not too heavy
for me to move. The wheels are part
of a folded-up wheelchair.

I try to pull the sides apart, but they're stuck
together. I try again, but they don't move.
Then I tug with all my might,
and the chair opens.

I push it back to where Grandma is sitting.

"Thank you, Thomas. Now I'll need
my slippery board to change wheelchairs."

Grandma keeps her slippery board by the red chair
in the living room so she can slide into that chair.
Nate and I have lots of fun sitting on the board,
scooting across the carpet.

I get the board, and Grandma slides
from her broken wheelchair into the old one.
I push the old wheelchair down the driveway.
It works fine.

When Nate comes from school, we all go into the kitchen. Grandma heats some soup.

Nate sits in a chair.
Usually I eat lunch on Grandma's lap,
but today I feel like sitting in a chair, too.

"I have my own special seat at kindergarten," Nate says.
"You have to be five years old to go to kindergarten."

"I don't care," I tell him.
"When you go to school, I go to Grandma's house.
Her lap is a special seat for one four-year-old—me!—
whenever I need it."